TOM GROSS

HI THERE, WALDO FRIENDS!

I'M OFF ON ANOTHER FANTASTIC JOURNEY, AND YOU CAN COME ALONG! THIS TRAVEL BOOK IS FILLED WITH FUN, FACTS, AND TOMFOOLERY TO KEEP YOU ENTERTAINED. THERE IS ALSO SPACE WHERE YOU CAN WRITE ABOUT YOUR OWN TRAVELS WHEREVER YOU GO—NEAR OR FAR—THERE'S PLENTY TO EXPLORE BETWEEN THESE PAGES.

YOU'LL EVEN GET A BONUS SET OF SENSATIONAL STORY CARDS. JUST SHUFFLE THE CARDS AND GO. WHO KNOWS WHAT CRAZY CAPERS ARE ON THE OTHER SIDE! AND DON'T FORGET TO SEARCH FOR ME! I'M HIDING IN EVERY SCENE. FANTASTIC!

THERE'S LOTS OF FABULOUS FUN ALONG THE WAY, SO WE BETTER GET GOING. LET THE EXPEDITION BEGIN!

Waldo

SUITCASE SCRAMBLE

I've written a packing list of everything
I'm taking on my travels, but it's all muddled up!
Can you unscramble the words below?

KWAGLIN TSIKC	
ANOATRCI	
TETLEK	
STUHHRBOTO	
KBIUOODEG	
TRAWE BETLTO	
LOBNUCISAR	
EPLEGINS GAB	
PPMOOM AHT	

CHECKLIST FOR ADVENTURE

Fantastic! You better write your own checklist,
too! What are you taking on your adventures?

....

....

....

....

....

....

....

....

....

....

MORE THINGS TO FIND

Someone with heavy suitcases
A hat with a green feather
A man in a suit with red boots

AIR TICKET

BOARDING PASS

Where are you off to? What will you be doing there?
Write your plan of action below!

I'm going to ....

....

....

I am going with ....

....

....

I'm looking forward to ....

....

....

I am traveling by ....

....

....

Draw your vehicle of choice in the space below!

MORE THINGS TO FIND

- A jumbo jet
- A flying fish
- A paper bear-plane

7

HAPLESS HITCHHIKING

Oh, dear! It looks like this hitchhiker has taken a wrong turn and ended up at a wild party! How did he get there? You decide! Write his story in the space below!

I wtN Trch raNgt r shtsN

MORE THINGS TO FIND

- [ ] A pogoing punk
- [ ] Foxes doing the fox-trot
- [ ] A nervous-looking man in a tuxedo

Why not add these crazy characters to your story?

TREACHEROUS TRAINS

Something's gone offtrack in this strange station!
Spot ten differences between the two scenes below.

AT THE STATION

AT THE STATION (AGAIN)

TRANSPORT TANGLE

At the airport, everyone is in a hurry to refuel! But which truck is fueling each vehicle? Follow the lines below to find out!

TRAVEL TWISTER

Pack your bags—it's time to go! Can you find all
the terrific travel words that are hidden? They
go backward, forward, up, and down!

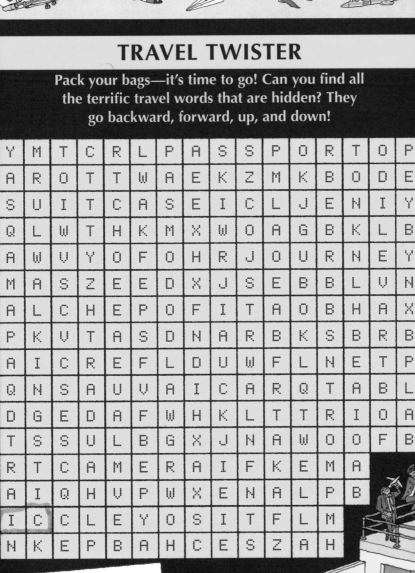

Y	M	T	C	R	L	P	A	S	S	P	O	R	T	O	P
A	R	O	T	T	W	A	E	K	Z	M	K	B	O	D	E
S	U	I	T	C	A	S	E	I	C	L	J	E	N	I	Y
Q	L	W	T	H	K	M	X	W	O	A	G	B	K	L	B
A	W	V	Y	O	F	O	H	R	J	O	U	R	N	E	Y
M	A	S	Z	E	E	D	X	J	S	E	B	B	L	V	N
A	L	C	H	E	P	O	F	I	T	A	O	B	H	A	X
P	K	V	T	A	S	D	N	A	R	B	K	S	B	R	B
A	I	C	R	E	F	L	D	U	W	F	L	N	E	T	P
Q	N	S	A	U	V	A	I	C	A	R	Q	T	A	B	L
D	G	E	D	A	F	W	H	K	L	T	T	R	I	O	A
T	S	S	U	L	B	G	X	J	N	A	W	O	O	F	B
R	T	C	A	M	E	R	A	I	F	K	E	M	A		
A	I	Q	H	V	P	W	X	E	N	A	L	P	B		
I	C	C	L	E	Y	O	S	I	T	F	L	M			
N	K	E	P	B	A	H	C	E	S	Z	A	H			

WORDS TO SEARCH FOR

BOAT • CAMERA • CAR •
JOURNEY • MAP • ODLAW •
• PASSPORT • PLANE •
SUITCASE • TRAIN • TRAVEL
• WALKING STICK • WOOF

BARKING BOATS

Woof here! Even hounds like me need a vacation, so I've come to the seaside! Can you spot the sea-themed silhouettes in the scene below?

12

MORE THINGS TO FIND

- A Viking ship
- A lobster bed
- A cowboy riding a seahorse

13

SEASIDE STORY

There are so many fascinating things at the beach!
One curious character is this wandering cowboy who's
lost his way. I wonder what his story is. Why don't
you decide? I've started the first sentence for you:

POOR STIRRUP STAN HAD NO IDEA HOW HE'D

STUMBLED ONTO THE SAND ....

....

....

....

....

....

....

....

....

....

....

....

....

THINGS TO THINK ABOUT

- Where did the cowboy come from?
- How will he get back?
- Will anyone help him?

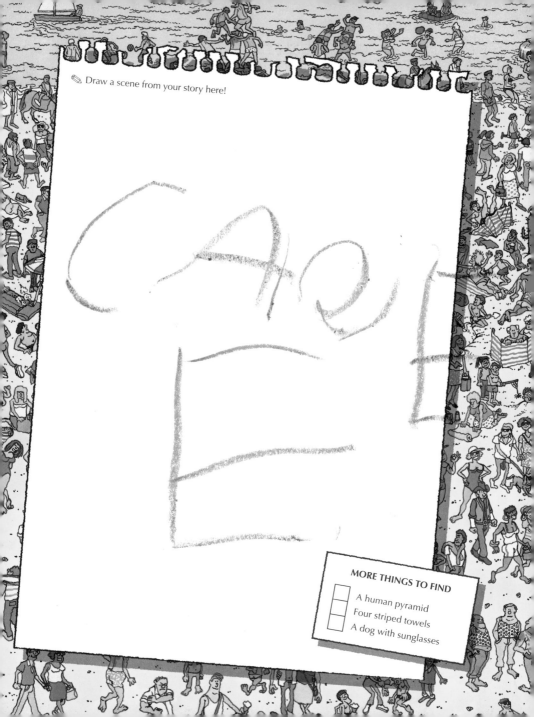

✎ Draw a scene from your story here!

MORE THINGS TO FIND

- [ ] A human pyramid
- [ ] Four striped towels
- [ ] A dog with sunglasses

MESSAGE IN A BOTTLE

Find seven real words or phrases by matching up the pairs of papers. Write your answers in the bottle below. You can use each piece more than once, and four pairs of ripped edges fit together perfectly.

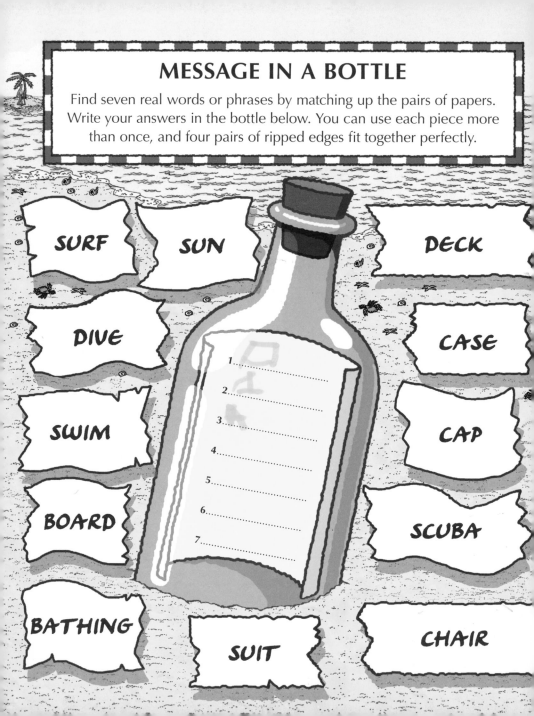

SURF

SUN

DECK

DIVE

CASE

SWIM

CAP

BOARD

SCUBA

BATHING

SUIT

CHAIR

1.
2.
3.
4.
5.
6.
7.

PATH OF THE PLUNDERING PIRATES

Can you navigate through these stormy seas and reach the desert island?

❶ **Start** by the man in yellow pants standing on one leg. Walk along the mast pole, but beware of the cannonballs! ❷ **Climb down** the shroud net without bumping into the brawling shipmates. ❸ **Hop along** the deck and say hello to Woof (all you can see is his tail!), then follow the pirate with a cutlass in his mouth up to the first crow's nest.

❹ **Take a right** along the middle mast and climb the rope to the top. ❺ **Leap onto** the mast of the skull-and-crossbones boat. ❻ **Swerve around** the three pirates gawking at Tarzan. ❼ **Head toward** the swinging gorilla, then zip-line down past the collapsing sail to the bowsprit. ❽ **Slide down** toward the drinking pirates, then shuffle to the very edge. ❾ **Time to** take the plunge! Call a mighty "Y'ARGHHH!" then dive into the deep blue sea and swim as fast you can toward the desert islands. Watch out for sharks!

THE PIRATE DIARIES

Imagine you're a pirate sailing the seven seas. Write what you did each day in the spaces below. Did you find buried treasure? Take on the kraken? You decide!

MONDAY

TUESDAY

WEDNESDAY

MORE THINGS TO FIND

- A pirate surfing
- A deflected cannonball
- A human ladder
- A yellow feather
- Exhausted rowers

20

THURSDAY ....

FRIDAY ....

SATURDAY ....

SUNDAY ....

WHAT AN EXPRESSION!

Wenda here! My photos have come out funny!
Can you complete the unfinished portraits?
Then draw your own in the empty frames.

22

FLYING HIGH

Time to visit the land of the dragon flyers!
Can you spot ten differences between the two pictures?

FEROCIOUS FLIGHT

These daring dragons are off on a vacation.
But where will they go? Use the space below
to write about where you think they're headed.

THINGS TO THINK ABOUT

- What are the dragons' names?
- What's in their luggage?
- Are they headed somewhere hot or cold?

Draw your own picture of a dragon here.

FLIP FLOP SILHOUETTES

Sit opposite a friend and see who can be first to match the silhouettes to the scene!

A B C D E

FLIP FLOP SILHOUETTES

Sit opposite a friend and see who can be the first to match the silhouettes to the scene!

A B C D E

CLOWN-TASTROPHE

Oh, dear! It looks like this Clown Town cyclist got a bad deal on this set of wheels. He started a complaint letter to the bike shop, but can you help him finish it?

Dear Jester or Joker,

There seems to be some funny business going on! One minute I was cycling along, happy as a clown can be, and the next ... POP! My wheels had turned square!

Yours in red-nosed fury,

MORE THINGS TO FIND

- Three thrown pies
- A car with eyes
- A clown watering his head

SILLY STAMP SNAP

Now it's time to mail some postcards.
Can you match each postmark to its stamp?

EGYPT

MUSKETEERS

ROBIN HOOD

MEDIEVAL

OUTER SPACE

JAPAN

CLOWNS

WALDOS

AZTECS

ROME

MORE THINGS TO FIND

- Six balloons
- A ticklish man
- An upside-down mummy sarcophagus

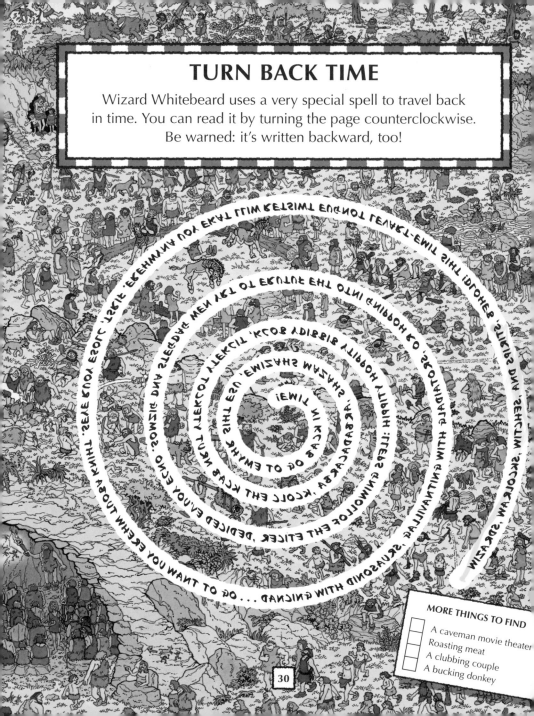

TURN BACK TIME

Wizard Whitebeard uses a very special spell to travel back in time. You can read it by turning the page counterclockwise. Be warned: it's written backward, too!

MORE THINGS TO FIND

- A caveman movie theater
- Roasting meat
- A clubbing couple
- A bucking donkey

30

TIME TO BUILD A MACHINE

Did the spell not work? Never mind . . . design your own time machine in the space below, and don't forget to label everything to show how it works!

✎ Draw your time machine here!

MEDIEVAL MAGIC

We've gone all the way back to the Middle Ages! See if you can spot these colorful characters in the scene:

MORE THINGS TO FIND

- A back-to-front knight
- A juggling jester
- A band of minstrels
- An angry fish

33

THE TERRIFIC TEMPLE TREK

Can you find the secret hiding place of the Aztec gold hoard? Follow the directions below.

❶ **Start your journey** by finding a Spanish conquistador holding a flag with a double-headed eagle on it. ❷ **Walk along** the base of the pyramid and climb up the tower of soldiers until you reach the man with the very tall red-and-orange feather headdress. Be careful not to get hit on the head! ❸ **Climb over** to the stairs at his right and run up to the platform at the top. Greet the man with the staff.

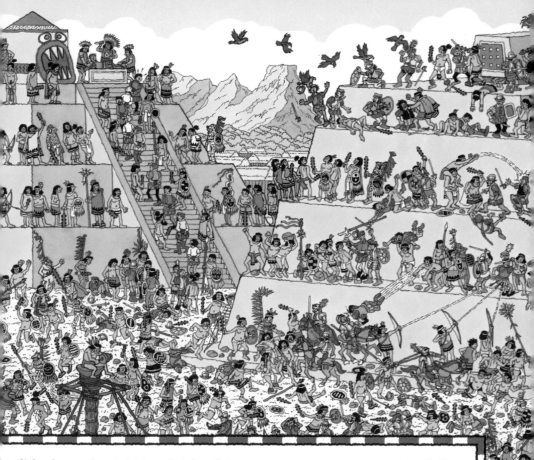

Slide down the right-hand side of the stairs. Once you get past the falling rock, see if you can find the man with closed eyes holding a crossbow in one hand. **❺ At ground level** walk to the right and find an Aztec warrior holding a yellow-and-black striped shield (do you think he knows Odlaw?). **❻ Crawl over** to another dropped yellow-and-black striped shield. Avoid the falling man! **Jump onto** the gray horse and let the helmeted rider trot you around the corner. **❽ Tiptoe up** the stairs to the top. **❾ Dash into** the open mouth without being seen!

MORE THINGS TO FIND

- Nine birds
- Thirty shields with feathers
- A man covering his ears
- Three men wearing gold medallions
- A pickpocket
- Eleven men in yellow costumes with black spots

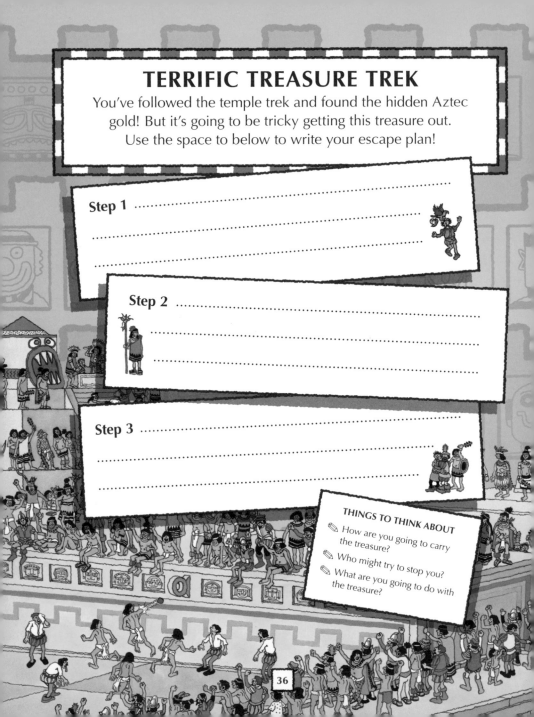

TERRIFIC TREASURE TREK

You've followed the temple trek and found the hidden Aztec gold! But it's going to be tricky getting this treasure out. Use the space to below to write your escape plan!

Step 1 ....

....

....

Step 2 ....

....

....

Step 3 ....

....

....

THINGS TO THINK ABOUT

🖊 How are you going to carry the treasure?

🖊 Who might try to stop you?

🖊 What are you going to do with the treasure?

36

Step 4 ....
....
....

Step 5 ....
....
....

✎ Draw your treasure here!

WRITE LIKE AN EGYPTIAN

Decode the ancient message using the scroll of hieroglyphics.
Then write your name in code using the blank scroll.

a	b	c	d	e	f	g	h	i	j	k	l	m

n	o	p	q	r	s	t	u	v	w	x	y	z

VERUM AUT FALSUM?

We've roamed all the way back to ancient Rome! Test your knowledge and work out whether these facts are true or false:

I. THE ROMAN EMPIRE WAS THE LARGEST EMPIRE IN HISTORY.

II. NEMESIS WAS THE ROMAN GODDESS OF REVENGE.

III. SACRED GEESE SAVED ROME IN 390 BCE.

IV. JULIUS CAESAR WAS AN EMPEROR.

V. ACCORDING TO LEGEND, THE FOUNDERS OF ROME WERE RAISED BY A WOLF.

VI. THE ROMANS WORE TOGAS EVERY DAY.

VII. CONCRETE WAS INVENTED BY THE ROMANS.

VIII. PLUTO WAS THE ROMAN GOD OF THE UNDERWORLD.

IX. DORMICE WERE A DELICACY SERVED AT BANQUETS.

X. ONLY MEN COULD BE GLADIATORS.

Turn to the back to check your answers!

MORE THINGS TO FIND

- [ ] A sad lion
- [ ] An emperor assassin
- [ ] Twenty-two red shields

ODLAW'S I-SPY!

Greetings, fellow troublemakers! I, Odlaw, love being a sneaky spy and spotting things on my vacations. Can you find all the things I've spotted in this spooky scene?

ODLAW'S I-SPY!

- ☑ A witch going the wrong way
- ☑ A witch riding upside down
- ☑ A dancing executioner
- ☑ A vampire holding a teddy bear
- ☑ A ghost train
- ☑ A sore finger
- ☑ A broom riding a witch
- ☑ Two prisoners catching two executioners
- ☑ A vampire holding a bat

Now it's your turn! Write your own checklist below of things to find in the world around you! Here's a few to start:

- [ ] A storm cloud
- [ ] A red traffic light
- [ ] An ice-cream cone

- [ ] ....
- [ ] ....
- [ ] ....
- [ ] ....
- [ ] ....

41

WHO DONUT?

Someone has eaten Waldo's birthday cake! Who could it have been? Read the testimonies below, then see if you can guess who the crumb-filled culprit is.

IT WAS A BEAUTIFUL SUNNY SUNDAY, SO I WENT FOR A BIRTHDAY STROLL, THEN CAME BACK TO MEET MY PALS FOR THE PARTY. BY THE TIME I ARRIVED, THE CAKE WAS ALREADY GONE!

I was wrapping Waldo's birthday present, which is tricky when you only have paws! I asked Odlaw for help when he snuck past, but he said he was busy. By the time I was ready to fetch the cake, there were only crumbs left. . . .

I WAS OUT AT THE POST OFFICE PICKING UP WALDO'S BIRTHDAY CARDS AND PRESENTS. BY THE TIME I GOT BACK, THE PARTY HAD ALREADY STARTED, AND THE CAKE WAS GONE. I BET THEY ALL ATE THE CAKE TOGETHER WHILE I WAS AWAY!

I was in my magical workshop all morning making a birthday surprise for Waldo. Odlaw popped in to see if he could help but I said no—it's not a good idea to let someone so diabolical near my spell books!

I SPENT THE MORNING HANGING UP DECORATIONS FOR THE PARTY. THE CAKE WAS IN THE KITCHEN NEXT DOOR. I THINK I MIGHT HAVE HEARD THE DOOR OPEN AND CLOSE, BUT I WAS TOO BUSY BLOWING UP BALLOONS TO GO CHECK!

43

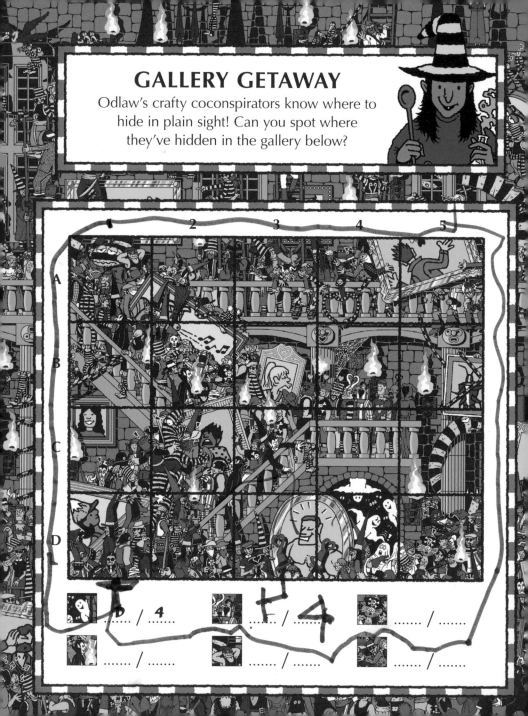

GALLERY GETAWAY

Odlaw's crafty coconspirators know where to hide in plain sight! Can you spot where they've hidden in the gallery below?

MENACING MUG SHOT

Imagine you're a brilliant detective and you've just brought in your chief suspect. Fill in their rap sheet below and draw their mug shot!

CRIMINAL RECORD

Name: ....

....

Date of Arrest: ....

Confession*: YES / NO

Hair*: Black / Brown / Blond / Red / Green / Bald

Eyes*: Brown / Blue / Green / Hazel / Purple / Yellow

*CIRCLE AS RELEVANT

Details of Crime: ....

THE EnD STUF
AloT ThoO WeW FT. Te

....

....

THINGS TO THINK ABOUT

- How did you catch them?
- Do they have any distinctive features?
- Do they have any special skills?

GOING UNDERGROUND

Match the silhouettes to the people and creatures in these terrifying tunnels. Make sure the monsters don't gobble you up!

MORE THINGS TO FIND

- A ladder
- A snake with a spear
- Ten hidden coins

HI THERE, TRAVEL LOVERS!

NOW IT'S TIME FOR <u>YOU</u> TO GET WRITING! THESE
PAGES ARE FOR YOU TO RECORD ALL YOUR FAVORITE
MOMENTS FROM YOUR JOURNEY. MY FRIENDS AND
I HAVE ADDED IN A FEW FUN PROMPTS TO GET
YOU STARTED, BUT THEN IT'S TIME TO GO ALONE.
GOOD LUCK, WALDO FANS—AND HAVE FUN!

Today's date is ....

Where did you go today?   What was the weather like?
What was your favorite thing you saw?

....

....

....

....

....

....

....

....

....

....

TRAVEL CHALLENGE

Can you find someone wearing stripes? Bonus points if the stripes are red and white like Waldo's!

MORE THINGS TO FIND

- Hitchhikers
- A flying saucer
- The Milky Way

Today's date is ....

Where did you go today?   Who did you go with?
What did you have to eat?

....

....

....

....

....

....

....

....

....

....

....

TRAVEL CHALLENGE

Try a new food! Ask a
parent or guardian for
help picking one.

MORE THINGS TO FIND

- A fishing fish
- A sawfish
- A sea lion

Today's date is ....

Where did you go today?   What did you do there?

Who were you with?

....

....

....

....

....

....

....

....

....

....

....

TRAVEL CHALLENGE

Find out how to say these
phrases in a foreign language:

Hello! • Happy travels!
• Have a good day!

MORE THINGS TO FIND

A hungry lion
A crouching tiger
A cheetah in love

Today's date is ....

Where did you go today?   What did you see?
Did you take pictures?

....
....
....
....
....
....
....
....
....
....

TRAVEL CHALLENGE
Can you crack this coded message? Cross out the Xs between the other letters.

HXXEXLXLO WAXLXDXOX FXAXNXS! XHXAVXE AX FXAXNTXASXTIC DXXAXYX!

MORE THINGS TO FIND
- A popping balloon
- A skydiver
- A paper airplane

Today's date is ....

Where did you go today?   Did you take anything with you?

What made you smile?

....
....
....
....
....
....
....
....
....

TRAVEL CHALLENGE

Try to use the following words in a conversation without your friends or family noticing!

Dinosaur • Waldo • Pineapple

MORE THINGS TO FIND

- [ ] A ticklish monster
- [ ] A monster with a sword
- [ ] A spear-munching monster

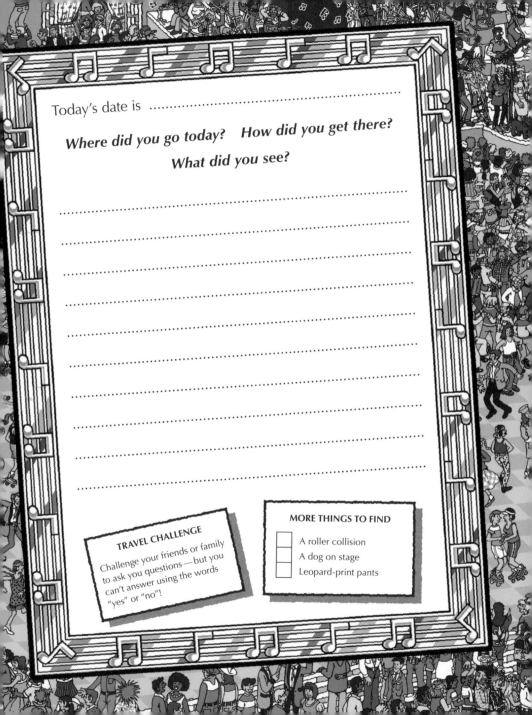

Today's date is ....

Where did you go today?   How did you get there?
What did you see?

....

....

....

....

....

....

....

....

....

TRAVEL CHALLENGE
Challenge your friends or family to ask you questions—but you can't answer using the words "yes" or "no"!

MORE THINGS TO FIND
☐ A roller collision
☐ A dog on stage
☐ Leopard-print pants

Today's date is ....

Where did you go today?   Did you meet anyone new?
What was the best thing you did?

....

....

....

....

....

....

....

....

....

....

TRAVEL CHALLENGE

Practice saying the alphabet backward to impress your friends and family.

MORE THINGS TO FIND

- Two beastly bands
- A scared vampire
- A mummy nurse

Today's date is ....

Where did you go today?

Was it far away?

Did you listen to any music?

....

....

....

....

....

....

....

....

TRAVEL CHALLENGE

Create your own pirate name! Your first name could be your favorite color, and your last name could be your favorite sea animal (e.g., Pirate Green Shark!).

MORE THINGS TO FIND

☐ Two seagulls
☐ A sea bath
☐ Someone walking the plank

Today's date is ....

Where did you go today?   Did anything surprise you?

What was the best moment?

....

....

....

....

....

....

....

....

....

....

TRAVEL CHALLENGE

Each image in the gold frames comes from somewhere in this book! Can you find them all?

MORE THINGS TO FIND

- [ ] A falling ladder
- [ ] Two witches
- [ ] A picture of a bear

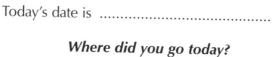

Today's date is ....

Where did you go today?
Did you play any games?
Did anything make you laugh?

....

....

....

....

....

....

....

....

....

TRAVEL CHALLENGE

Find out a fun fact
about where you are
traveling!

MORE THINGS TO FIND

☐ A pair of unhelpful firefighters
☐ Two spacemen
☐ Four cats

Today's date is ....

Where did you go today?   Did you get any souvenirs?

If you could have invited anyone to be with you, who would it be and why?

....

....

....

....

....

....

....

....

....

TRAVEL CHALLENGE

Write a letter to your future self telling them about your trip.

MORE THINGS TO FIND

☐ A Stone Age wheel
☐ Three shields
☐ A dragon

CRAZY CHARACTER CONSEQUENCES

Tear out the perforated pages to play a wacky
Waldo game of consequences with your pals!

Here's how it works:

1. Each player takes a piece of paper.

2. On your piece, write down a character on the first line.

3. Fold the paper over what you've written so the next
    person can't see what it says.

4. Pass the folded paper along to the right and take the
    paper from the person to your left.

5. Write another character using the prompt on the second
    line, then fold it again as before.

6. Repeat this process until everyone has a complete story
    like the ones Wenda, Wizard Whitebeard, Odlaw,
    and I made — you can see them on the next page.

Name: Al the Alien

met: Superstar Stevie

at/~~in~~/~~on~~: a pirate ship.

One said: Quick! Now's our chance to escape!

The other replied: I come in peace.

And then: they both tripped on the carpet.

Name: Treasure-Hungry Harry

met: Effra the Elephant

~~at~~/in/~~on~~: outer space.

One said: Can I have your autograph?

The other replied: It's mine, you scurvy dog!

And then: the zookeeper found them.

Name: Zev the Zebra

met: Anita the Astronaut

~~at~~/~~in~~/on: the red carpet.

One said: Yargh! Where's me treasure?

The other replied: Toot, toot!

And then: they set off to a new planet.

Name: Camera-Carrying Caz

met: Peg-Leg Patty

at/~~in~~/~~on~~: the zoo.

One said: Gargle, bleep, bloop!

The other replied: Of course, *darling*!

And then: they fought with cutlasses.

MORE THINGS TO DO

Can you work out the original stories before they got swapped around?

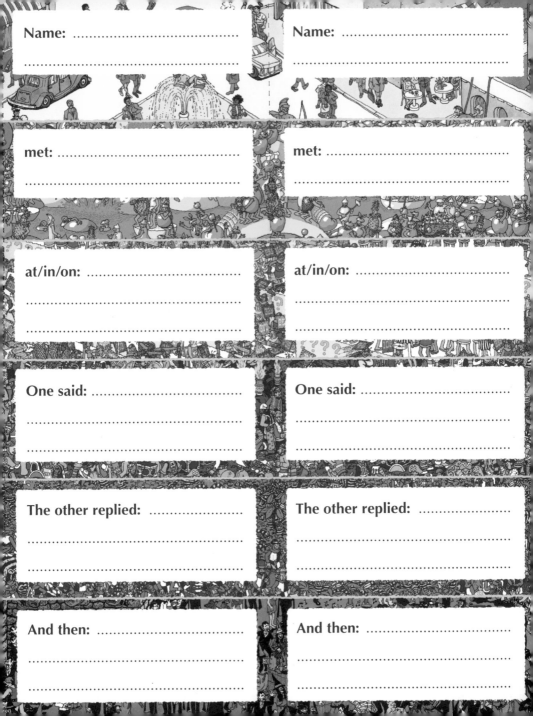

Name: ....
....

met: ....
....

at/in/on: ....
....
....

One said: ....
....
....

The other replied: ....
....
....

And then: ....
....
....

Name: ....
....

met: ....
....

at/in/on: ....
....
....

One said: ....
....
....

The other replied: ....
....
....

And then: ....
....
....

MORE THINGS TO FIND

- Falling papers
- A harp swing
- A pirate invasion

MORE THINGS TO FIND

- Swept-up notes
- A broken light
- Tap dancers

Name: ....

....

Name: ....

....

met: ....

....

met: ....

....

at/in/on: ....

....

....

at/in/on: ....

....

....

One said: ....

....

....

One said: ....

....

....

The other replied: ....

....

....

The other replied: ....

....

....

And then: ....

....

....

And then: ....

....

....

MORE THINGS TO FIND

- Three dice
- Blue 181
- A Hula-Hoop

5+4=9

2+2=7

MORE THINGS TO FIND

- A rocket
- Pink 506
- Maize in a maze

Name: ....

....

met: ....

....

at/in/on: ....

....

....

One said: ....

....

....

The other replied: ....

....

....

And then: ....

....

....

Name: ....

....

met: ....

....

at/in/on: ....

....

....

One said: ....

....

....

The other replied: ....

....

....

And then: ....

....

....

MORE THINGS TO FIND

- [ ] Two red horses
- [ ] A shield being stomped on
- [ ] A blue man in a pink shirt

MORE THINGS TO FIND

- [ ] A flag running
- [ ] A shirtless red man
- [ ] A red-and-white horse

Name: ....
....

Name: ....
....

met: ....
....

met: ....
....

at/in/on: ....
....
....

at/in/on: ....
....
....

One said: ....
....
....

One said: ....
....
....

The other replied: ....
....
....

The other replied: ....
....
....

And then: ....
....
....

And then: ....
....
....

MORE THINGS TO FIND

A pool table
Tennis elbow
A baseball bat

MORE THINGS TO FIND

Home plate
A long bow
Snow-peaked caps

WELL, WHAT AN ADVENTURE! I HOPE YOU HAD AS MUCH FUN AS I DID. BUT DON'T GO JUST YET: THERE'S STILL MORE FUN TO BE HAD! I LEFT MY OWN TRAVEL JOURNAL SOMEWHERE ON THE PAGES OF THIS BOOK. LOOK AT THE IMAGE BELOW AND THEN TURN BACK TO SEE IF YOU CAN FIND IT!

TRAVEL JOURNAL

AND THERE'S MORE! THERE ARE A WHOLE HOST OF STORY GAME CARDS IN THE FRONT AND BACK OF THIS BOOK FOR YOU TO USE WITH YOUR FRIENDS OR MAKE YOUR OWN FUN!

Waldo

ANSWERS

P. 4 SUITCASE SCRAMBLE

KWAGLIN TSIKC – WALKING STICK

ANOATRCI – RAINCOAT

TETLEK – KETTLE

STUHHRBOTO – TOOTHBRUSH

KBIUOODEG – GUIDEBOOK

TRAWE BETLTO – WATER BOTTLE

LOBNUCISAR – BINOCULARS

EPLEGINS GAB – SLEEPING BAG

PPMOOM AHT – POM-POM HAT

P. 10 TRANSPORT TANGLE

P. 11 TRAVEL TWISTER

				P	A	S	S	P	O	R	T		
S	U	I	T	C	A	S	E						
	W						J	O	U	R	N	E	Y
M	A										V		
A	L			O		T	A	O	B		A	R	T
P	K			D							R		
	I			L		A		C	A	R	T		
	N			A		W							
T	G						W	O	O	F			
R	T	C	A	M	E	R	A						
A	I				E	N	A	L	P				
I	C												
N	K												

P. 16 MESSAGE IN A BOTTLE

Some options include: 1. SCUBA DIVE;
2. DECK CHAIR; 3. SWIMSUIT;
4. SUITCASE; 5. SUNBATHING;
6. SURFBOARD; 7. SWIM CAP

P. 30 TURN BACK TIME

Wizards, warlocks, witches, and spirits, behold! This time-travel tongue twister will take you anywhere. First, close your eyes. Think about where you want to go . . . dancing with dinosaurs, gallivanting with gladiators, or into the future to try new gadgets and gizmos. Once you've decided, recite the following spell: Hippity hoppity bibbidy bock, tickety tockety turn back the clock, abracadabra shazam shazime, use this rhyme to go back in time!

P. 38 WRITE LIKE AN EGYPTIAN

Find a crocodile face! Then find a crocodile elsewhere in this book! Make it snappy!

P. 39 VERUM AUT FALSUM?

1. False; 2. True; 3. True; 4. False; 5. True; 6. False; 7. True; 8. True; 9. True; 10. False

PP. 42–43 WHO DONUT?

Odlaw stole the cake! He said he was out all morning but Woof and Wizard Whitebeard both saw him. And there's no mail on Sundays!

First U.S. edition 2019

ISBN 978-1-5362-0670-8

18 19 20 21 22 23 WKT 10 9 8 7 6 5 4 3 2 1

Printed in Shenzhen, Guangdong, China

This book was typeset in
Optima and Wallyfont.

The illustrations were done in ink and
watercolor or in ink and colored digitally.

Candlewick Press
99 Dover Street
Somerville, Massachusetts 02144

visit us at www.candlewick.com

ONE FINAL THING . . .

The fun and games aren't
over! The cards at the
front and back of this book
are pieces to a puzzle.
Can you put the scene
together, and then find
Waldo? Happy hunting!

CRAZY CREATIVITY CARDS

Pick six cards, any six cards . . .

Now's your chance to create your own stories, using the story cards at the front and back of the book as prompts.

Draw six cards from the pack at random and shuffle them.

There are six different prompts: Characters (x2), Places, Props, Actions, and Challenges.

Now make your story with **CHARACTER ONE** from the first card, **CHARACTER TWO** from the second card, the **PLACE** from the third card, the **PROP** from the fourth card, and the **ACTION** from the fifth card. Then, if you're feeling brave, take the **CHALLENGE** from the sixth card!

So, for example, you might end up with something like:

Tell a story that includes:

1. Who: Waldo

2. And: A vampire

3. Where: At the beach

4. With: A magic scroll

5. Doing what? Throwing a surprise party.

6. But you have to . . . Add in sound effects!

***Waldo** went to the **beach** to **throw a surprise party** for a **vampire**. But Waldo forgot that vampires can't go out in the sun. Luckily, Waldo found a **magic scroll** in the sand. Waldo recited the magic words written on the scroll. **Zap! Crash! Whoosh!** The spell conjured up a giant umbrella to block the sun! With the umbrella to protect him, the vampire had a great time at his party!*

Are you ready? Let's play!